CRUISIN'

Motocross Cycles

By S.X. Carser

PUBLISHED BY
Capstone Press
Mankato, Minnesota USA

CIP
LIBRARY OF CONGRESS CATALOGING IN PUBLICATION DATA

Carser, S.X. (Sharon X.) 1954-
    Motocross cycles / by S.X. Carser
       p. cm. -- (Cruisin')
    Summary: Describes how motocross motorcycles differ from regular motorcycles, how they should be selected, and how they are properly and safely used.

    ISBN 1-56065-069-9:
    1. Motocross–Juvenile literature. [1. Motocross.]
    I. Title. II. Series.
    GV1060.12.C37 1989
    796.7'56--dc20   89-27868
                                                        CIP
                                                        AC

Photo Credits:
Kinney Jones: 3, 4, 6, 8, 9, 11, 12, 13, 14, 15, 16, 19, 20, 21, 22, 24, 26, 27, 28, 30, 32, 33, 35, 36, 37, 38, 41, 42, 43

Cheryl Blair: 17, 18, 44

Copyright ©1992 by Capstone Press, Inc. All rights reserved. No part of this book may be reproduced in any form without written permission from the publisher, except for brief passages included in a review. Printed in the United States of America.

Capstone Press
P.O. Box 669, Mankato, MN, U.S.A. 56002-0669

CONTENTS

Around the World on an MX Cycle 7

More Than a Motorcycle 10

The Engine 14

Off the Road 20

How Do You Choose the
Best MX Cycle For You?....................................23

Safety First 26

Riding Skills 32

Minibikes Can Motocross Too!...........................36

Glossary 39

Index 45

AROUND THE WORLD ON AN MX CYCLE

The name motocross is really two words made into one. "Moto" comes from the French word, **motocyclette**. And "cross" comes from **cross-country**.

At first, MX racing took place only in Europe. In 1947, a French man named Roland Poirer set up the first motocross race. Because many nations took part in the race, it was called *Motocross Des Nations.* That means "motocross of the nations." This event still takes place every year.

Drivers raced cycles that carried the names of Norton, Triumph, BSA, BMW, FN, or Husqvarna. These are names of the companies that made the machines. All are European companies.

The first MX cycles used in racing were the large 500cc (cubic centimeters) size. Two British companies, Norton, and BSA, and the Belgian company FN, made some of the best MX cycles. For nearly ten years, one of these MX cycles won the race.

These MX cycles were heavy and sometimes too powerful. Soon, race drivers wanted MX cycles that were easier to handle. The Swedish company, Husqvarna, began making a 500cc MX cycle that was lighter and easier to control.

In the 1960s, MX racing was becoming popular in the United States. As the sport grew, race drivers began driving lighter and less powerful MX cycles. Japan also responded to this new demand. They began making good MX cycles in the 125cc and 250cc size categories.

Today, European companies are not making the most popular MX cycles. Japanese companies with names like Suzuki, Honda, Kawasaki, and Yamaha make the best selling cycles in the USA and around the world.

MX cycles are now made all over the world. Let's find out how they are made and where to find them.

MORE THAN A MOTORCYCLE

All motorcycles are not the same. Some are small, others are big. Some go faster than others do, and some motorcycles have special uses. One use is racing.

Maybe you have seen a motorcycle race. The most exciting kind of motorcycle racing is **motocross**. Motocross racing is hard and demanding. This sport is so demanding that special machines are made for it. These machines are called **motocross motorcycles**. Professional racers call them MX cycles.

Motocross races take place on permanent tracks. These tracks are called courses. Each course must be between one and three miles long. Motocross race courses have many natural and man-made road blocks. The blocks can be highspeed jumps, muddy areas, sharp turns, or steep hills.

All of the drivers start the race at the same time. The race is divided into two parts called **heats**. Each heat may last as long as 40 minutes. The MX racer must finish a set number of laps around the course in a short amount of time. The winner is chosen after the times from both heats are added together. A race driver may not do well in the first heat, but can still win the race by doing well in the second heat.

MX cycles with bigger engines go faster. That is why motocross races are divided into three classes. These classes are decided by the size of the MX cycle's engine.

There is a class for engines that are 125cc. A class for 250cc engines, and a class for 500cc engines. (Cubic centimeter is a scientific way of measuring how big

something is. Right now just remember that the more cubic centimeters (cc's) an engine has, the bigger and more powerful it is.) An MX cycle with a 500cc engine is four times more powerful than an MX cycle with a 125cc engine. You can see why it would not be fair if they all raced together.

Where does this power come from? Let's look inside the MX cycles.

THE ENGINE

The engine on the MX cycle works like other motorcycle engines. Almost all motorcycles are powered by gasoline-fueled **internal combustion** engines.

An MX cycle engine usually has one **cylinder**. A cylinder looks like a long hollow tube. Inside this tube is a **piston**. A piston is a kind of plug that fits inside the cylinder.

The piston is connected to the **crankshaft** by a long rod. The piston can move up and down inside the cylinder. Everytime the piston moves, the crankshaft turns once.

One end of the cylinder is open. This is the end where the piston goes. The other end of the cylinder is closed except for two **valves**. The valves open and close. One valve controls the flow of gas into the cylinder. The other valve leads to open air. Burned gas, called **exhaust** escapes from this valve.

The area inside the cylinder is measured in cc's. Sometimes this number is part of a motorcycle's name (like the Honda 250). That way, the buyer knows right away how large the engine is. For example, a small minibike will have a 50cc engine. The smallest MX cycles have a 125cc engine. The smallest MX is 2 1/2 times more powerful than a minibike!

Engines In Motion

The piston's power comes from a mixture of gasoline and air. When you turn the key into the **ignition**, the engine starts. At the same time, the engine sucks in the mixture of gasoline and air. Remember, this comes through the valve and into the cylinder.

Starting the engine sends electricity to the **spark plug**. The spark plug is at the closed end of the cylinder. Electricity makes a spark and starts the fuel on fire.

The fuel and air mixture inside the cylinder burns very fast. Heated air expands and pushes the piston down as far as it can go. The piston begins moving up again, and the exhaust valve opens. As the piston moves up it pushes the burned gas out of the cylinder. This process is called the **power stroke**.

The power stroke makes the MX cycle run. MX cycles have a 2-stroke engine. With each stroke, the crankshaft makes one complete turn.

The process repeats over and over again as long as the engine is turned on. You stop the flow of electricity to the spark plug when you turn the key that shuts off the engine.

Power Train

The **power train** connects the rear wheel to the crankshaft. (Remember that the crankshaft is connected to the piston by a long rod.) The power train has three parts, a **clutch**, a **gearbox**, and a **chain**. As we will see, each part has a special purpose.

The Clutch

A clutch is made up of two groups of metal plates. These plates go around in circles. One group of plates connects to the engine. The other group connects to the power train. When the cycle is moving, the plates are pushed together by a big spring. When the cycle is at rest, the plates are apart.

When the clutch is **engaged**, it connects the engine to the powertrain. When it is **disengaged**, the clutch separates the engine from the powertrain. Disengaging the clutch lets the engine run when the cycle is not moving.

Gears

Put the fingers of your right hand between the fingers of your left hand. See how your hands are now locked together in this position? That is how **gears** work. All gears have fingerlike parts called teeth. The gearwheel teeth fit into the links of a chain. Once the gear and the chain are hooked together, they move each other in a circle.

Gears control how fast the motorcycle wheels turn. MX cycles have five or six gear positions. By moving the **gearshift lever**, you select the proper gear setting.

You have probably changed gears while riding your bicycle. It's the same when you change gears on an MX cycle. The gearshift levers on an MX cycle are located on the right handlebar grip. Every time you move the gearshift lever, the chain moves to a different gear. Depending on whether you shift up or down, the cycle will go faster or slower.

When starting out or going up a steep hill, "first" gear is used. This is the slowest speed and will give the most power. To go faster, shift into higher gears. Once at top speed, there is no need to change gears again. Change gears only if you come to a steep hill or need to stop.

Unlike your bicycle gears, MX cycle gears are covered by a box. This is the gearbox.

Drive Chain

MX cycle engines are in the middle of the motorcycle. The clutch is next to the engine, and the gearbox is next to the clutch. The rear wheel is about 12 inches away from the engine. A chain is used to connect the gears to the rear wheel. This is called the **drive chain**.

OFF THE ROAD

You may sometimes hear MX cycles called "trail bikes" or "dirt-bikes." That's because they are made for loose dirt race tracks. MX cycles cannot be driven on paved roads. They are not as fast or as heavy as road motorcycles either.

MX cycles cover rough land, and so they are built differently from other motorcycles. For example, the exhaust pipe is placed high on the MX cycle's frame. There it won't hit the ground when the cycle goes over bumps and rocks. The front wheel fender is high above the wheel, so it won't become clogged with mud.

MX cycles do not have horns, lights, or mirrors, because they are not driven in traffic. But they do have heavy duty tires. These tires have big knobs, called knobbies, that can grip in the loose dirt and mud.

HOW DO YOU CHOOSE THE BEST MX CYCLE FOR YOU?

Choosing a cycle depends on many different things. It depends on how big you are. Or whether or not you are an experienced motocross racer. Most racers want an MX cycle that would help win a race, like the Motocross Des Nations. But those types of MX cycles are not for sale.

Let's say that the winning MX cycle of the Motocross Des Nations 250cc race is a Honda 250. You can be sure this is a very special MX cycle. Honda made it specially for one driver. This is a one-of-a-kind MX cycle. This is known as a factory-sponsored racer.

But not everyone is interested in winning the Motocross Des Nations. Just to try motocross racing, a cycle needs to match your size and racing abilities.

Most beginners start out with a 125cc MX cycle. This is the smallest MX cycle. There are lots of 125cc motocross races, so you will be able to use this cycle often. The more you ride your MX cycle, the better you will get at racing.

You may like the 125cc cycle so well that you will never want a larger bike. You will become a better driver with practice and then you might want to try a 250cc MX cycle. If you are big and bold enough, you may even move up to a 500cc cycle.

You must be prepared to buy some spare parts for your MX cycle. Even the strongest machines break sometimes. So when you buy a cycle from a dealer, always ask how much repair costs are. For example, it helps to know how much a new piston or fender would cost.

Adjustments

Most MX cycles need to be adjusted before they are ready to ride on the race track. Most are easy to do.

You do not have to buy a bike just because the handlebars fit you the best. Handlebars are easy to raise or lower. It is important to remember that handlebars should be placed low. Then you can put the weight of your body over the front wheel.

You may also want to change your handlebar grips, depending on the size of your hands. The grips may need to be fatter or skinnier. They should also be soft to provide comfort throughout a long race.

Your new bike may come with plastic fenders. If not, replace the metal fenders with plastic ones. Plastic fenders may break, but metal fenders bend and get jammed against the tire.

The chain is the hardest part to manage on your MX cycle. Sometimes a chain falls off during a race. It is very hard to put back on, so the chain must be greased often to move smoothly.

Dirt clings to a greased chain and makes the chain wear out faster. Or worse, dirt causes the chain to break. So clean and regrease the chain regularly. Also, because it loosens easily, the chain needs to be adjusted often.

Be sure to check all the nuts and bolts on your MX cycle.

SAFETY FIRST

Even the smallest MX cycles are very powerful. Powerful enough to make your cycle jump many feet into the air. That is why it is important to develop good racing habits.

While learning these good habits, you are going to take some spills. Don't worry, this happens to everyone. You need to learn how far to push before your cycle goes out of control. It is at these times that you will need good safety equipment.

When MX cycle racers are dressed in their safety equipment, they sometimes look like football players! The drivers wear a cotton jersey padded at the chest. Their leather pants are padded at the knee and thigh. Boots are also made of leather and padded. Every driver wears a helmet, goggles and gloves.

Helmet

You will need to start out with a good helmet. Check to see if the helmet you want is certified by the Safety Helmet Council of America (SHCA). This group tests helmets. If your helmet has a SHCA sticker on it, you know it's been through some tough testing.

While you're looking for the SHCA sticker, also check the padding inside the helmet. The padding should be all over the inside. There should be two kinds of padding. One is very soft, like a cushion, because it fits against your head. Under that padding, a stiff material is glued to the helmet. The force of a blow is absorbed by this stiffer padding.

The helmet must fit snugly. If it moves around on your head it cannot do its job. In fact, all your equipment should fit you well. Don't borrow boots and gloves from someone else.

Goggles

It is important to protect your head and face. Choose goggles that fit snugly. Goggles prevent dirt and rocks from flying into your eyes. Also, a visor attached to your helmet gives you extra protection.

Boots

Boots used for MX cycle racing have a steel liner under the rubber sole. These boots also have steel toes, because your feet often get dragged along the track during a race. Under these conditions, even the strongest leather tears apart.

An MX cycle engine gets very hot during a race. To protect your calves from this heat, your boots should be 15 to 16 inches high. Tuck your pants into your boots. Now dirt and rocks cannot get inside them.

Pants

Your pants should be made of leather. Cowhide is good, but it gets very hot during the race. Goatskin pants are preferred by European race drivers. Goatskin pants are lighter, and they allow you to move more freely. They are cooler too.

Whether you choose cowhide or goatskin, your pants must be padded at the knees and hips. Sweat stiffens leather. A good set of leather pants can be washed in cold water. Afterward oil the pants to keep them soft.

Shirt

It's too hot to wear leather jackets or vests during motocross races. A long-sleeved shirt made of cotton, or nylon is best. Wear the shirt over a padded chest protector.

Gloves

A good pair of leather gloves protect your hands during a race. They give you a better grip on the levers and handlegrips too. Good gloves help you to control your bike better.

RIDING SKILLS

The Wheelie

A wheelie is done by lifting the cycle's front wheel about one foot off the ground. Professional MX cyclers call wheelies "popping it."

A racer will lean towards the back of the cycle, turn the **throttle** to speed the engine up, and gently pull back on the handlebars. The cycle will continue to move forward as the driver balances on the back wheel.

It may seem that a wheelie is only a show-off trick. But wheelies also make it possible to jump over big rocks or logs. Once the front wheel has cleared, the back wheel will roll over the rock. Wheelies will carry a racer over a rock that is up to one foot tall!

The Standing Position

The standing position is not as hard to learn as the wheelie. In fact, all the racer does is stand on the footpegs instead of sitting on the seat. But it is one of the most important skills to have in MX cycle riding.

When shifting weight while riding, standing helps to control the cycle. The legs also become shock absorbers in this position. Sometimes it's more comfortable to stand when riding over some rough areas.

Spinning the Donut

Spinning donuts means making a tight, sliding circle in loose dirt. An impression of a donut is left behind. It is an important stepping stone to learning other racing skills.

To begin, the racer moves the cycle slowly forward in first gear, sliding the left foot along the ground and moving the cycle to the left. At the same time, the racer puts more weight on his left foot and now increases speed.

As the racer moves faster, the front wheel stays in one place. At the same time, the back wheel begins to lift up and circle around. The front wheel becomes the center point of the circle. (Or the hole of the donut.)

Once a racer has learned this skill, they will have developed an important MX cycle riding ability. For example, spinning the donut allows you to change directions very quickly.

The Brake Slide

Brake slides are done when a racer needs to make a fast stop. By stepping on the rear brake and holding it, the rear wheel locks and the cycle slides sideways and stops. With practice, a good racer should be able to do a brake slide at fast speeds, stopping in a sideways position.

When a racer becomes an advanced MX cycler, they combine the brake slide stop with the donut. This movement is called the power slide. But that is for the advanced rider.

35

MINIBIKES CAN MOTOCROSS TOO!

You are probably thinking: "yes, motocross sounds great, but it will be a long time before I get to ride. I'm too small for even the smallest MX cycle." Well, part of that may be true. But you can try motocross racing on a smaller cycle.

Minibikes are a small version of an MX cycle. Minibikes can do a lot of the things an MX cycle can do. The difference is that minibikes are smaller and less powerful.

A club called National Youth Project Using Minibikes (NYPUM) started in Los Angeles, California, 20 years ago. In this club, members learn how to ride and take care of a 50cc minibike. Boys and girls between the ages of 10 and 15 may join. As you can tell by the name, NYPUM is a national organization. So there may be a club in your city.

In a NYPUM club, you will learn basic riding skills. You also learn how to repair a minibike. They will teach you to follow all of the strict safety rules.

Are you interested in joining a club like this one? Find out if there is a NYPUM club near your home. A good place to check is with your local YMCA. These clubs are popular, and many kids want to join. In some cases it may be hard to get in. But if you want to begin experiencing the world of MX cycles, it is well worth trying!

SCOTT
PEAK
36
JEROMY
BUEHL
Coors
LIGHT
HONDA
PRO CIRCUIT
CAMEL
SUPERCROSS
RENTHAL
RENTHAL
36
SUPERCROSS
SPARK PLUGS
HONDA
36
PRO CIRCUIT
CAMEL
PRO CIRCUIT

GLOSSARY

Clutch: This is made of two metal plates: One plate is connected to the engine, the other is connected to the powertrain.

Crankshaft: The shaft is connected to the piston and to the powertrain.

Cross-country: An English word meaning across country.

Cubic Centimeters: A method of measuring the space inside the cylinder.

Cylinder: Shaped like a tube, this hollow part of the engine is where gasoline is burned.

Disengage: When the clutch is disengaged, the engine is not attached to the powertrain.

Drive-chain: A system that includes a large chain connecting the gears and the rear wheels.

Engage: When the clutch is engaged, the engine is attached to the powertrain.

Frame: This structure holds the cycle together. For example, the handlebars, wheels and seat are connected to the frame.

Gears: These moving parts, with grips called teeth, join with a chain that is attached to the rear wheels. (See drive-chain.)

Gear-box: A box that contains the gears, it is also called the transmission.

Gearshift lever: Located on the left handlebar grip, this lever engages and disengages the clutch.

Heats: A motocross race is divided into two or three parts. Each part is called a heat.

Ignition: This process starts the fuel on fire inside the cylinder.

Internal Combustion Engine: An engine, fueled by gasoline, burns and expands inside a cylinder.

Motocross: A special type of motorcycle racing that takes place on a closed, loose-dirt track. The race track also contains many roadblocks.

Piston: This plug, inside the cylinder, pushes burned gas out of the engine. When the piston moves up and down, the crankshaft also moves.

Power train: This connects the gears, clutch, and chain to the rear wheel.

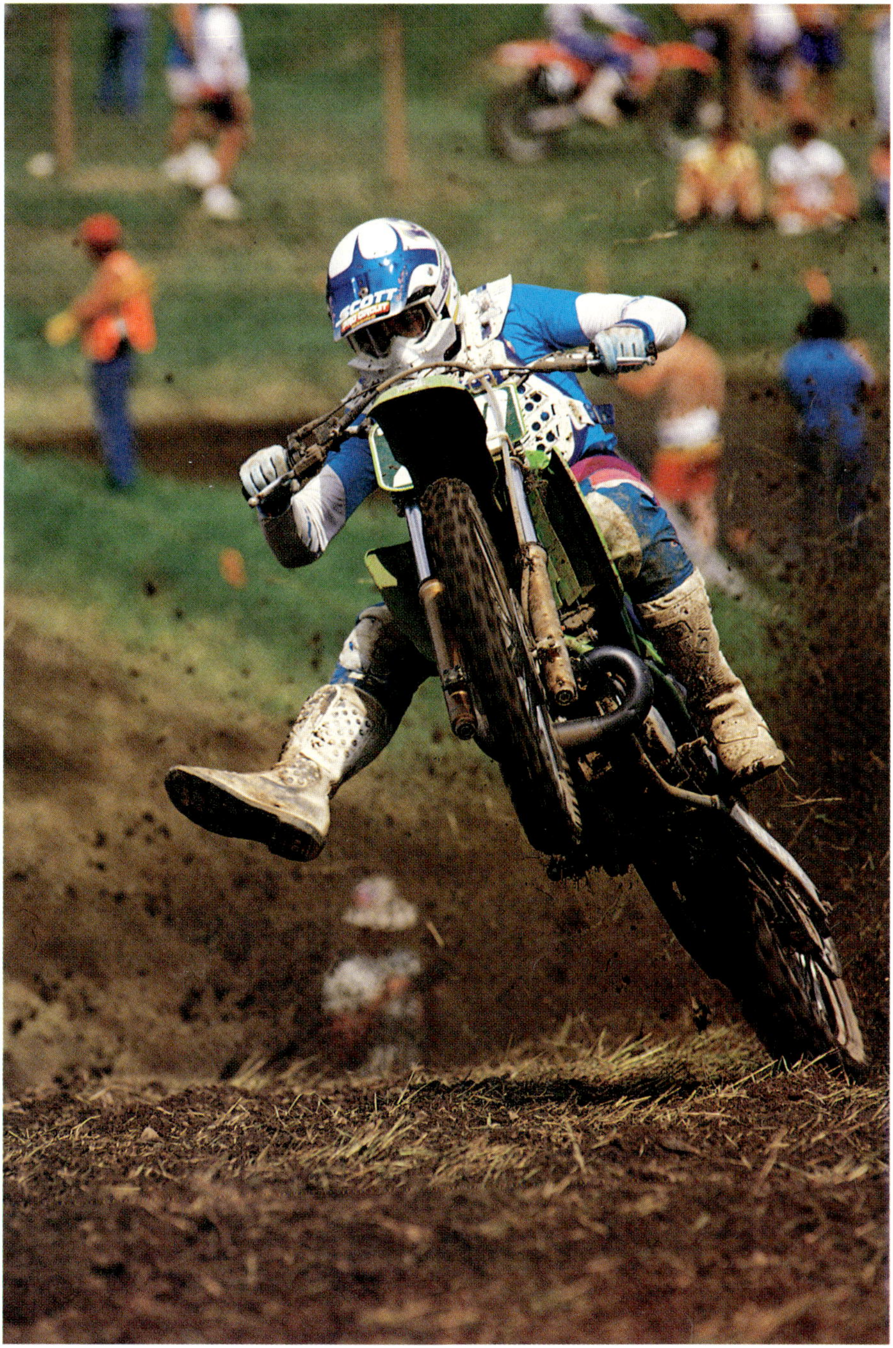
SCOTT

42

Spark plug: A small part located at the top of the cylinder, the spark plug receives an electric charge causing it to make sparks. These sparks start the gasoline inside the cylinder on fire.

Throttle: The throttle controls how much gasoline goes from the gas tank into the cylinder. The throttle is part of the right handlebar grip.

Valves: The two openings of the cylinder allow gasoline in and exhaust out.

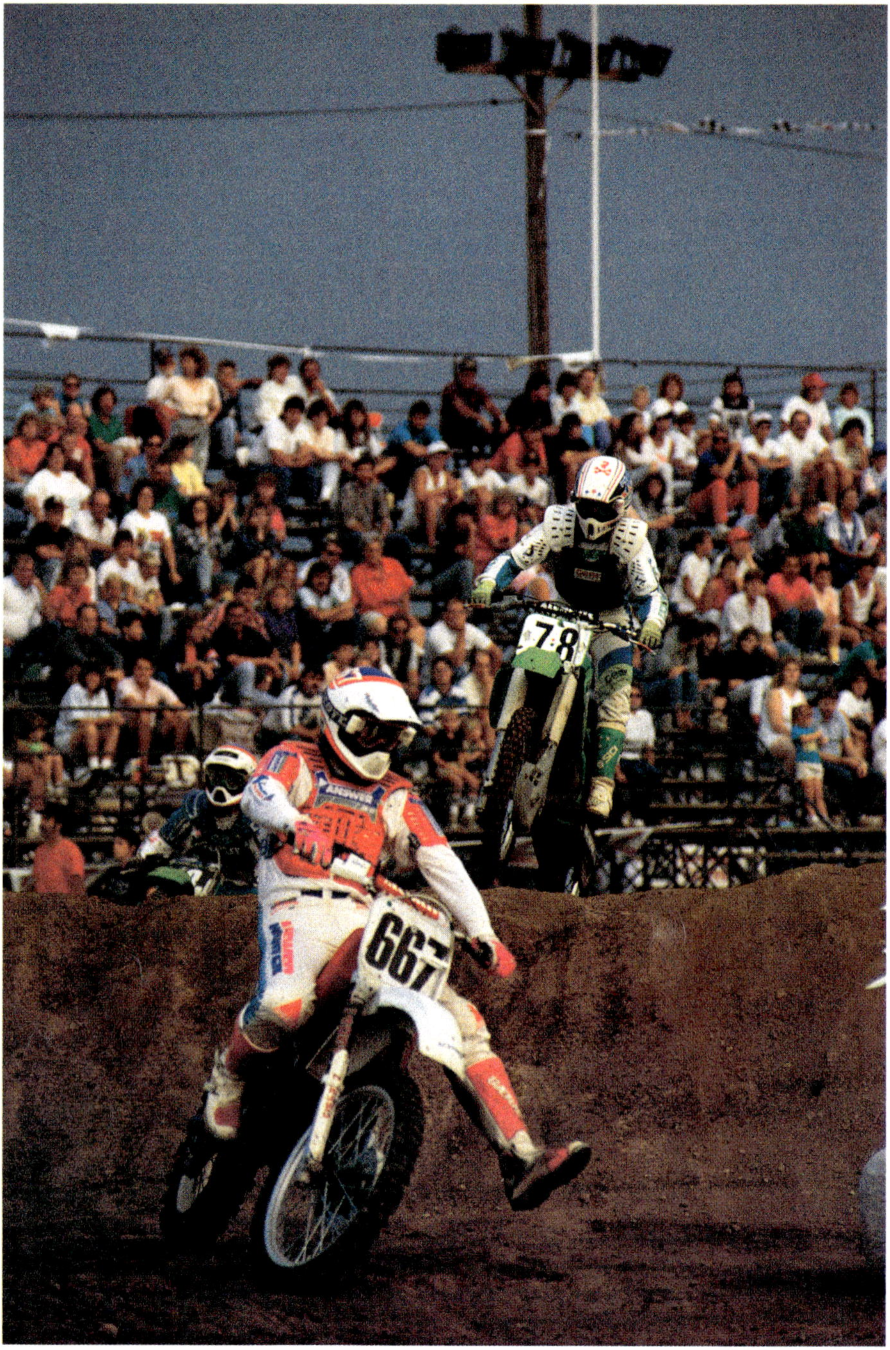
78
667

INDEX

BMW	7
boots	27, 29
Brake Slide, Brake Slides	34
BSA	7
chain	17, 18, 19, 25
clutch	17, 19
crankshaft	14, 16, 17
Cubic centimeter, cubic centimeters, cc, cc's	7, 11, 13, 15
cylinder	14, 15, 16
dirt-bikes	20
drive chain	19
electricity	16
engine, engines	11, 13, 14, 16, 19, 29, 32
engine, 2-stroke	16
exhaust	16
exhaust pipe	21
fender, fenders	21, 25
50cc	15, 37
500cc	7, 11, 13, 23
FN	7
foot-pegs	33
fuel	16
gasoline	16
gasoline-fueled	14

gear, gears	18, 19, 34
gearwheel	18
gearbox	17, 19
gearshift lever	18
gloves	27, 29, 31
goggles	27, 29
greased	25
grips	25
handlebar, handlebars	18, 25, 32
heat, heats	10
helmet, helmets	27, 28, 29
highspeed jumps	10
Honda	8, 15, 23
Husqvarna	7
ignition	16
internal combustion	14
Kawasaki	8
knobbies	21
knobs	21
metal plates	17
Motocross Des Nations	7, 23
National Youth Project Using Minibikes (NYPUM)	37
Norton	7
125cc	8, 11, 13, 15, 23
pants	27, 29, 31
piston	14, 15, 16, 17
Poirer, Roland	7
power slide	34

power stroke	16
power train	17
Riding Skills	32, 37
safety equipment	27
Safety Helmet Council of America (SHCA)	28, 29
shirt	31
spark plug	16
Spinning the Donut	34
spring	17
standing position	33
Suzuki	8
throttle	32
tire, tires	21, 25
trail bikes	20
Triumph	7
valve, valves	15, 16
wheelie, wheelies	32, 33
Yamaha	8